Goldilocks and the Three Bears

Retold by Russell Punter

Illustrated by Lorena Alvarez

Once there was a little girl named Goldilocks.

She looked like a little angel...

but she was really a little **trouble maker**.

She was naughty from first thing in the morning...

all through the day...

to last thing at night.

And she never, **ever** did as she was told.

"Please go and get some bread from the village,"
said Goldilocks' mother one day.

"Go straight there," she added firmly.

"I will," sighed Goldilocks.

But Goldilocks soon wandered off.

She saw smoke billowing from the chimney of a thatched cottage.

"What a funny little house," she thought.

She pressed her face
against the window.

"No one at home," she
thought with a grin.

She pushed open the front
door, and a terrifically tasty
smell wafted out.

Goldilocks skipped inside.

There on a table were
three bowls of porridge.

Ahhhhh!

First she tried the
biggest bowl.

Her face flushed bright red.
"Too hot!" she gasped.

Then she tried the
middle-size bowl.

"Ooo!" cried Goldilocks.
"Too cold!"

Last of all, she tried
the little bowl.

It was the yummiest,
scrummiest porridge
she'd ever tasted.

Slurp! Burp!

"What next?"
she thought.

In front of the crackling
fire were three chairs.

First she tried the
biggest one.

"Too hard!" she said,
rubbing her sore bottom.

Then she tried the
middle-size one.

Ooof!

"Too soft!" yelped Goldilocks, sinking into the squishy cushions.

Just right!

Last of all, she sat down firmly on the smallest chair.

Whoops!

But seconds later came a **snap!**

and the little wooden chair collapsed.

"I need a nap," yawned Goldilocks.

She ran up the stairs...

and came to a big, bright bedroom.

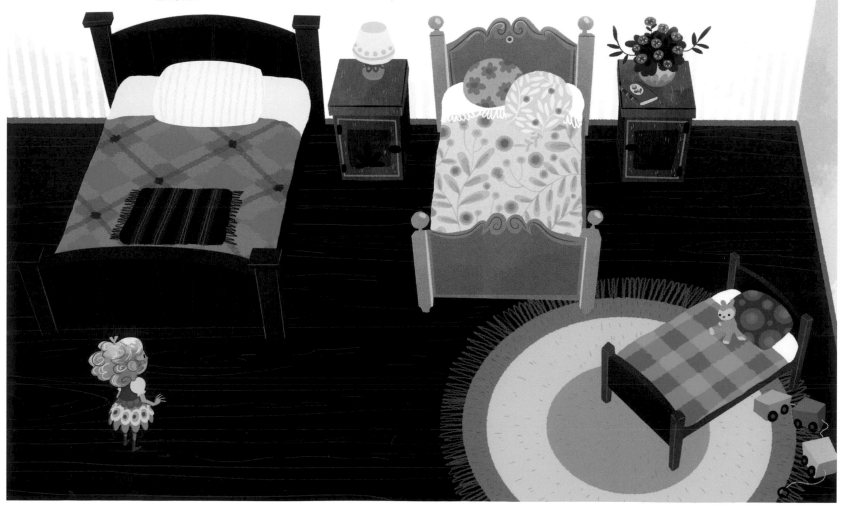

First she tried the
biggest bed.

"Too high!" she puffed,
out of breath.

Then she tried the
middle-size bed.

"Too deep!" she cried,
drowning in the
squashy mattress.

Help!

Last of all, she tried
the smallest bed.

She climbed on top and
rested her head on the
soft, downy pillow.

"Ah," she said.
"Just right."

Pulling the blankets up
to her chin, she snuggled
down and fell asleep.

Meanwhile, the owners of the house returned.

"Who left the front door open?" asked Father Bear.

"Not me, dear," said Mother Bear.

"Not me," echoed Baby Bear.

They went inside.

"Hey! Someone's been eating my porridge," grumbled Father Bear.

"Someone's been eating *my* porridge,"
sighed Mother Bear.

"And someone's been eating *my* porridge,"
sniffed Baby Bear, "and they've eaten it **all** up!"

Worse was to come...

"Someone's been sitting in my chair!" exclaimed Father Bear.

"Someone's been sitting in *my* chair," added Mother Bear.

"And someone's been sitting in *my* chair," wailed Baby Bear, "and they've **broken** it to pieces!"

Just then, they heard snoring.

The three bears followed the noise upstairs...

What a mess!

"Someone's been sleeping in my bed," boomed Father Bear.

"Someone's been sleeping in *my* bed," gasped Mother Bear.

"Someone's been sleeping in *my* bed," squealed Baby Bear...

"...and she's still in it!"

Goldilocks woke with a start to find
three grumpy bears glaring at her.

She leaped from the bed,
scrambled downstairs,
and raced outside.

She didn't stop running until she got home.

"I'm really sorry for not doing what I was told,"
Goldilocks said to her mother.

"I promise I'll never, **ever** be naughty again."

And she never was...

...well, *almost* never!

Edited by Lesley Sims

First published in 2015 by Usborne Publishing Ltd., Usborne House, 83-85 Saffron Hill,
London EC1N 8RT, England. www.usborne.com Copyright © 2015 Usborne Publishing Ltd.